Playing with words

This book belongs to

_____

Irene Babsky Dip. Ed. MA

LORENZ BOOKS

Irene Babsky is a teacher, singer and reviewer of children's books. She studied at the University of London Institute of Education and specializes in language acquisition, children's literature and English as a second language. She has worked as a primary school teacher in Britain and Africa. She now freelances as a teacher of children with special needs, as a storyteller and as an educational consultant advising schools on book provision and children's writing programmes.

contents

Learning Together

This book is divided into four topics, speaking skills, learning to listen, ready for reading and learning to write. These chapters reflect the Early Learning goals for the foundation stage of the Reception class and the National Curriculum and Literacy Strategy of Year 1. These strands of literacy form the basic tools for a child's later learning, allowing them to express themselves and to communicate with others.

The activities in this book will help you and your child to enjoy the enriching journey into literacy. Some of the activities are more difficult than others and you will need to assess your own child and focus on relevant activities. So, for example, if they are finding it difficult to write the letters of the alphabet, you could write letters and words for them occasionally until they gain confidence and mastery. Although the book can be dipped into, most children will find it easier and more enjoyable to start with speaking and listening. When a child has mastered a page, they can tick this off on the progress chart at the back of the book – but remember to continue to revisit all these newly mastered skills so that your child continues to extend and enjoy using language.

Early learning

In the early years at school, seeing and doing, listening and talking, are all part of the enjoyment of growing up, and you can help your child in this process.

Working with your child

Find a quiet, cosy place to look at the book together without any interruptions. Only spend a short time, for example 5 to 10 minutes, looking at the book and if the child wants to stop then let them. Learning is fun. Children are naturally curious and keen to find out more, but trying to push them too hard may put them off learning.

Other things to do with your child

You are your child's most important teacher, and they will learn more from you than from anyone else. Talk to your child whenever you are together, doing the chores at home, gardening, going shopping, travelling on a bus or out visiting. Encourage your child to talk about what they are seeing and experiencing.

Children's learning

Everyone learns at a different rate and often a child can do things that we consider difficult but can't do other things that we think of as easy. Encourage your child and make them see reading and writing as fun things to do.

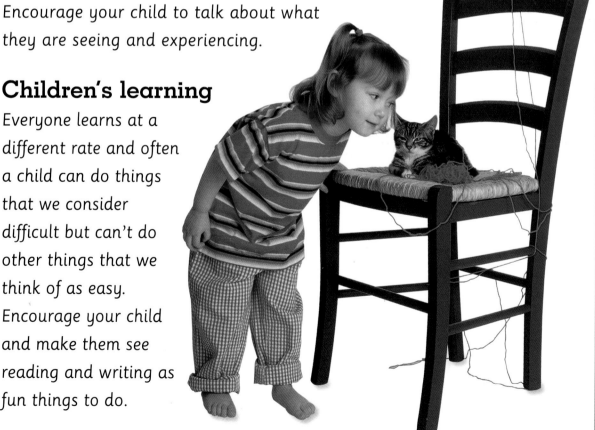

In this chapter you will learn the names of lots of things that you can find in the house and garden. You will sort things into different colours and shapes. You will talk about how you feel and practise telling stories about the things you like to do, such as dressing up and going to the park.

speaking skills

What can you see?

Jane and Claire are in the garden. They are very busy. What they are doing? What are they wearing? Talk about all the different things you can see on this page.

Now try this!

Can you sort some of the things you can see into groups? Sort all the red things into a group. Name all the different things that can grow. Name all the gardening tools.

Where does it go?

Can you help Emma put everything in the right room?
You might like to trace, colour and cut out the
different things so that you can move them
around and try them in different places.

Now try this!

Can you name all the different things that you have in your bedroom? Draw a picture of each of them and colour it in. Make a list.

Can you sort different things?

Anna is playing with her bricks. How many different colours of bricks does she have? Can you find things that are the same colour as some of her bricks?

These children are holding different shapes. Do you know what shapes they are? Can you find some other things on the page that are square shapes? Are there any circle shapes? What shape is this flag? Can you see anything that is the same shape as the flag?

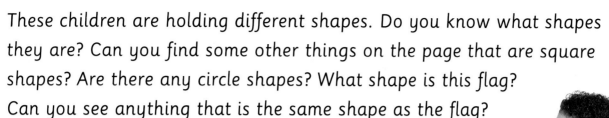

Now try this!

Can you cut some different shapes out of coloured paper and make a picture? Use squares, circles, triangles, rectangles and ovals. Now tell a friend all about your picture.

How do you feel?

James is thinking about what he and his friends are going to do today.
Do you think they would rather go to school or play football?

Things may happen to James and his friends that will make them sad or scared. How will they show their feelings? Who is sad? Who is happy? Can you match the right label to the right picture?

Now try this!

Look in the mirror and see how many different faces you can make. Try sad, puzzled, happy, angry and scared. Now try to make some silly faces.

sad

scared

happy

puzzled

Do you like dressing up?

These children are having fun choosing outfits from the dressing-up box. What are they dressed up as? Can you help them find the things they need to complete their outfits? Who do you think will need a wand? Who needs the pretty pink ballet shoes? Does anyone need sunglasses? Can you find the pirate's eye patch?

pirate

clown

Now try this!

Who would you like to dress up as? Make up a story about your favourite dressing-up outfit. Draw the things that you will need and talk about what happens.

cowboy

fairy

Where are they going?

It is the weekend and these children are going out for the day. Where do you think they are going? Will it take a long time to get there? Look at the pictures to find some clues.

Now try this!

Can you think of all the things you might need to go to the park? Draw the things and tell someone about the things you have chosen.

This chapter helps you learn to listen carefully and remember by making up stories. There are some fun games to play with your friends. You will learn which words begin with the same sound and which words sound like others.

Learning to Listen

Are you good at listening?

Can you help to fill a shopping basket by playing this game with some friends? The first person says, "I took my basket and put in some ... bananas." The next person says, "I took my basket, and put in some bananas ... " and then adds an item of their own. How many things can be added before someone makes a mistake?

Now try this!

Choose one of the items from the shelves. Get your friends to guess what it is. They can ask questions like, "Is it red?" or "Do you spread it on bread?" You can only answer "yes" or "no".

What happens next?

Peter has got himself dressed. Can you sort out the pictures so that they are all in the right order? What did Peter put on first? What is the last thing he put on? Tell a friend what you think. Does your friend think you are right?

Now try this!

Play this game with a friend. Say, "The owl and the pussy cat went to sea in a boat." Then your friend can add a new word. "The big owl and the pussy cat went to sea in a boat." Listen carefully to remember the new sentence. How many words can you add before one of you makes a mistake?

Can you make your own story?

There are lots of things on this page to help you make up a story. Cut out some cards to cover up the pictures. Begin the story, "One day the little girl/boy…". Then lift the first card and make up one or two sentences of your own. Have fun with some friends, taking it in turns to lift a card and add to the story.

Now try this!

Sit in a circle with some friends. The first person says, "I was walking on a beach and ..." As soon as they say "and", the next person has to carry on the story. "I was walking on a beach and found a magic bottle and ..." The last person has to finish the story.

What does it sound like?

Stephen is trying to find pairs of things that sound alike. Can you find two things that sound like 'look'? What other pairs can you find?

coat

cone

dog

mat

snail

fish

book

bee

pail

bear

frog

hat

dish

key

boat

hook

pear

bone

Now try this!

Play this game with a friend. Choose one of the objects on this page. Each person takes it in turn to say a word that sounds the same. Begin with mat, cat, sat ... How many more words can you add that sound the same as mat?

I spy with my little eye

George is playing a game of I Spy with Sally. They are taking it in turns to choose. George has chosen something that begins with the sound 'd'. Sally has guessed doll and duck. Can you think of anything else on this page that begins with 'd'? What can you see that begins with 't'?

drum   boat   top   clown

bear   doll   ball   books   dog

abc

skittles

frog

Now try this!

You can play I Spy with a friend. Say, "I Spy with my little eye something beginning with..." Choose something and say the sound it begins with. Ask your friend to guess what you spy.

telephone balloon duck

cat

Now you can start reading. In this chapter you will find words that have the same sound, as well as words for colours and numbers. You will learn how to use words to describe things. Then you will put words together to make sentences.

abc

ready for reading

Which is the right label?

Can you help Pippa to label the fruit on her stall? Look at the first letter and make the sound to help you choose the right label. Banana begins with 'b'. Can you find the label?

bananas

lemons

strawberries

oranges

apples

pears

grapes

Now try this!

Cut out some cards. Make two equal piles. Copy the name of a fruit on each card in one pile and draw a picture of each fruit on each of the other cards. Turn the cards face down and play a game of pairs with a friend. Take it in turns to pick up two cards to see if you have a fruit with the matching label. The one with the most pairs wins.

Words that have the same sound

There are lots of words on this page. Can you help Chloe match the labels to the pictures? Look at the first letter of the words to help you read the labels. What begins with 'c' or 'd'? If there is more than one label with the same first letter look at the last letter in the word to help you choose.

cap

cone

bear

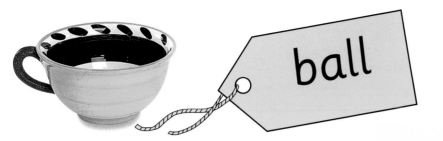

ball

dog

Now try this!

Make a word chain with a friend. The first person chooses a word. The second person has to think of a word beginning with the last letter or last sound of the first word. For example, cat … top … pig. The next word begins with 'g', and so on.

doll

cup

duck

box

Can you read colour and number words?

How many balls is Sophie juggling? Isn't she clever! What colour are the balls? What colour is the fish? How many skittles are there? Look at the groups of things on the page.

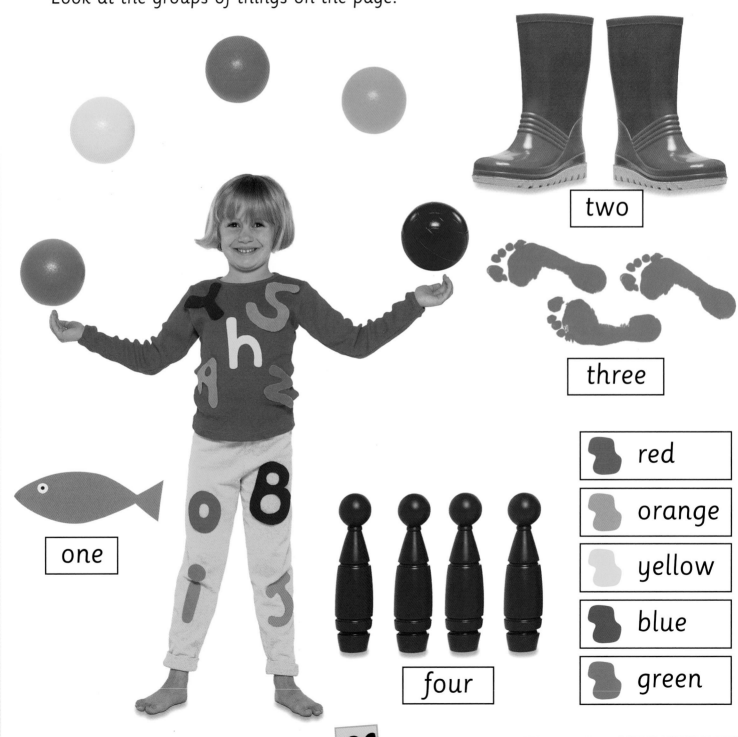

two

three

one

four

red

orange

yellow

blue

green

Can you join the words to make a sentence for
each of the pictures?

one	green	ducks
two	blue	fish
three	red	skittles
four	yellow	boots
five	orange	footprints

five

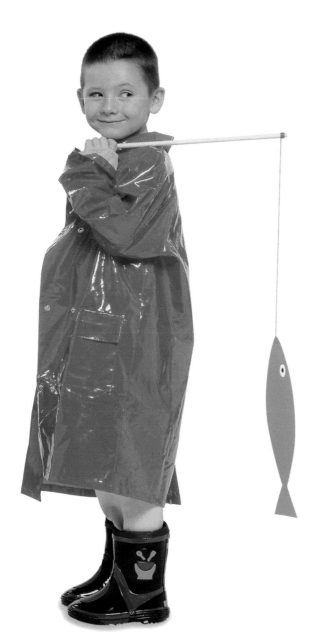

Now try this!

Do you know this rhyme?
Can you sort the lines into
the right order and read
them aloud?

Six, seven, eight, nine, ten

Once I caught a fish alive

Then I let it go again

One, two, three, four, five

Words that describe

Rosie has a big teddy and Amanda has a small teddy. The words big and small are describing words. Can you choose the right word to describe the things on this page? Put a tick in the box. The first one has already been done for you.

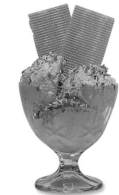

My ice cream is   cold ✔
hot

My hat is   dull
shiny

The teddy is fluffy
smooth

My chair is   hard
soft

These sentences have got muddled up.
Can you sort them out?

| dog | small | the | is |

| wet | coat | is | my |

Now try this!

Can you make some sentences of your own using the describing words on this page?

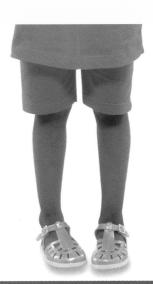

| is | yellow | my | ball |

What are these children doing?

These children are having fun. They are all doing different things. Who can hop? What can Tom jump over? Who is skipping with a rope? Read the sentences to find out.

| Tom | can | jump | over | the | bricks |

| Kay | can | skip | with | a | rope |

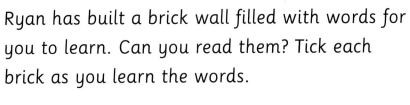

Ryan has built a brick wall filled with words for you to learn. Can you read them? Tick each brick as you learn the words.

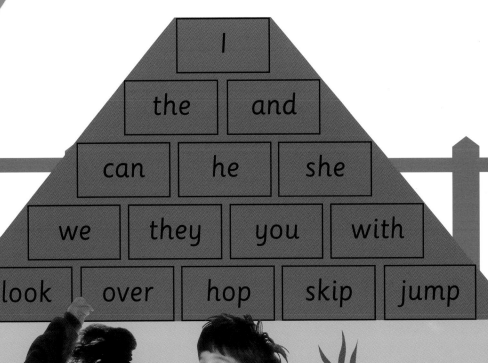

I

the and

can he she

we they you with

look over hop skip jump

Now try this!

Can you build some sentences of your own? Copy the words from the brick wall and arrange them in a row. Here is one to begin. "I can hop, skip and jump."

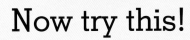

Suzy and Bill can hop

Can you read rainy day words?

Karen and Gemma are going for a walk with their friend Joshua. What are they wearing to keep themselves dry? Here is a story about the picture. Can you say the missing rainy day words?

clouds

umbrella

hat

coat

puddles

rainbow

boots

It is a **rainy** day.

Karen has a big bright ☐ .

Gemma is wearing a yellow ☐ .

She likes to jump in ☐ .

Joshua is pointing to the ☐ .

He is wearing red ☐ .

The sun is coming out from behind the ☐ .

Now try this!

Draw a picture of yourself on a rainy day. What would you be wearing? Use the words on this page to make up a story about what you would do on a rainy day.

In this chapter you will learn about writing all the letters of the alphabet, words, sentences and stories. You will find ideas for stories to write and lots of words to help you. Ask a parent to help you make a book or keep a folder so that you can read your stories to other people.

Learning to write

Can you write these words?

Luke is practising writing letters. He can write all the letters in the alphabet. Can you follow the arrows and draw over the dotted lines to write the alphabet too? Now write the words under these pictures. Do you know what the words say?

a b c d e f g h i j k l m n
o p q r s t u v w x y z

mat

hat

bin

key

tie

ball

frog

bag

mug

Now try this!

Draw some things that begin with the same letter. Write the name of each thing underneath. Here are some words that begin with 'd'.

dog   dish   door

Can you think of more words that begin with 'd'?

top

cup

49

What will you write in the box?

Do you like going to the park? These children are having lots of fun because there is so much to do. Can you read the questions and write the answers in the boxes?

kite

dog

bread

boots

a b c

tree

sun

clouds

bike

Now try this!

What do you like to do in the park? Write a story and draw a picture of yourself having lots of fun.

pond

ducks

What is Paul flying in the wind?

What is Susan taking for a walk?

What does Sam have for the ducks?

What is Laura riding?

What are swimming in the pond?

What does Sam have on his feet?

51

Can you write a list?

Judy and Ryan are having fun on the beach. They have brought lots of things with them so they can enjoy their day. Can you write a list of things that you would need to take for a day at the beach?

sea

sand

bucket

ball

goggles

sun hat

sunglasses

swimsuit

spade

sun

Now try this!

Have you been to the beach? Draw a picture and write a story about your day on the beach. Was it sunny? Did you go for a swim or a paddle? What do you like best about going to the beach?

bag

suntan lotion

swim ring

trunks

sandals

towel

Writing a recipe

David has made some cakes and Linda is going to decorate them. The instructions for icing the cakes have got muddled up. Can you help her sort them out? Read the instructions below and write them in the correct order on the recipe sheet.

- Put icing on the cakes

- Mix the icing sugar with water

- Put the sprinkles on the cakes

- Add some food colour

- Put a cherry on top

Recipe Sheet

 1

 2

 3

 4

 5

Now try this!

Why don't you make some cakes and decorate them? Then you can invite a friend to tea. Can you write an invitation to your friend? Remember to write the day and the time you would like them to come.

sugar

sprinkles

water

cherries

spoon

bowl

food colour

Now write a story

Anna, Robert and George are having a picnic in the garden with their teddies. Write a story about their picnic using the sentences on the page to help you. Where are they having a picnic? Is it a good day for a picnic? What will they eat? What did they bring to play with? Are they enjoying themselves?

teddy

tricycle

roller skates

cakes

Now try this!

Would you like to have a teddy bears' picnic? Who would you invite? Write a list of your friends' names and make a name badge for everyone who you'd like to come to the picnic.

tablecloth

car

Can you write a letter?

Zoe and Sam are the same age and their birthdays are on the same day. They have both been given presents by their friends. Can you work out which of the toys on the shelf are in Zoe's parcels and which are in Sam's?

Now try this!

Can you help Zoe and Sam write a thank you letter? When you've finished, put the letter in an envelope and write the address on the front. Draw a stamp in the top right-hand corner.

doll

Sam

Sam

TO Sam

Word cards

Photocopy this page and cut out the word cards. Use the cards to help you make sentences. Don't use all the cards at once. Pick out three or four cards and make a sentence. For example – I am big. I am small. Am I big? My brother is small.

I	my	mum	dad
is	big	small	am
like	see	want	teddy
		friend	cowboy
		brother	fairy
		sister	pirate
		wet	clown
		fluffy	cat
		happy	dog
		sad	book
		the	television
		a	fish

I	can	read

girl

boy

red

yellow

blue

green

orange

pink

can

when

why

have

you

bread

duck

rainy

puddles

boots

coat

hat

umbrella

clouds

sun

hop

walk

run

skip

over

jump

rope

read

to

and

lemons

grapes

apples

write

say

has

oranges

bananas

yogurt

my   book   is   big

Progress Chart

Record your progress here.
Place a tick in the box when you have completed each section.

When you have completed a chapter, fill out the certificate.

62

abc

certificate of achievement

Speaking

_____

is a brilliant
Early Learner!

abc

certificate of achievement

Listening

_____

is a brilliant
Early Learner!

abc

certificate of achievement

Reading

_____

is a brilliant
Early Learner!

abc

certificate of achievement

Writing

_____

is a brilliant
Early Learner!

This edition is published by Lorenz Books

Lorenz Books is an imprint of Anness Publishing Ltd
Hermes House, 88 – 89 Blackfriars Road
London SE1 8HA
tel. 020 7401 2077; fax 020 7633 9499
www.lorenzbooks.com; info@anness.com

© Anness Publishing Ltd 2002

This edition distributed in the UK by Aurum Press Ltd
25 Bedford Avenue, London WC1B 3A
tel. 020 7637 3225; fax 020 7580 2469

This edition distributed in the USA and Canada
by National Book Network, 4720 Boston Way
Lanham, MD 20706; tel. 301 459 3366
fax 301 459 1705; www.nbnbooks.com

This edition distributed in Australia
by Pan Macmillan Australia, Level 18
St Martins Tower, 31 Market St, Sydney, NSW 2000
tel. 1300 135 113; fax 1300 135 103
email customer.service@macmillan.com.au

This edition distributed in New Zealand by
David Bateman Ltd, 30 Tarndale Grove
Off Bush Road, Albany, Auckland
tel. (09) 415 7664; fax (09) 415 8892

A CIP catalogue record for this book is available
from the British Library.

Publisher: Joanna Lorenz
Managing Editor: Linda Fraser
Editor: Joy Wotton
Design: Alix Wood of Applecart
Photography: Jane Burton, John Daniels, John
Freeman, Robert Pickett, Kim Taylor, Lucy Tizard

The publishers would like to thank all the children
who appear in this book.

10 9 8 7 6 5 4 3 2 1